Look Before You Leap

Written by
Barbara Gensch

Illustrated by
Rosie Lin

Fame's Eternal Books, LLC
United States of America

I dedicate this book to my daughter, Tammy Maté-Peterson. As a Spanish Immersion Third Grade Teacher and author, she devotes her life to children, the Police, the Military, people of all cultures, and to her family. She, like I, hope to help this world become a better, kinder, safer place.

Barbara Gensch

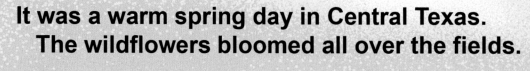

It was a warm spring day in Central Texas.
The wildflowers bloomed all over the fields.

There were blues, pinks, purples, and yellows.
A rainbow of colors.
The bluebonnets, the Texas state flower,
stood like miniature soldiers.

Out in the country, in a wooded backyard of a small home, the animals were waking up. The birds started to sing, the roosters to crow, hens to cluck, the baby goats to cry for their mama to feed them fresh, warm milk. Then came the loud braying of a donkey.

His name was **Shadow.** He could wake up the **whole neighborhood.**

A farm fence stood between two yards, and on the other side from where Shadow lived were two squirrels. They loved that yard, because it had a bird feeder. When the birds came to feed, they would scatter a lot of the seed on the ground for the squirrels to eat.

Many days, one of the squirrels would climb to the top of a huge, pointed rock that was near the bird feeder. He would take a flying leap, land on it; and then eat up all the delicious sunflower seeds and corn.

The man owner of the house would get upset, because he enjoyed seeing the mockingbirds, blue jays, cardinals, and other birds come to his feeder. So one day, he went out to the pointy rock, and spread it with a *gooey grease* that is used on *cars*.

That same day, the rock-climbing squirrel,

whose name was *Stump,* saw the lady of the house carry out a bucket of seeds to put in the empty feeder.

Stump's tummy rumbled, so he climbed to the top of the pointy rock. He felt surprised by something *gooey* on the bottom of his feet.

Suddenly Stump started to slide. **"OOOOH!"** He couldn't hold on, so he fell to the ground with a **thump.**

Stump's squirrel friend saw what had happened, and said, **"See, maybe next time you will have *patience,* and wait for the birds to scatter the seeds."**

The two squirrels loved to climb up on the roof of the house. The man and woman could hear their tiny feet scratching on the shingles. One day, Stump decided to jump on the roof while his friend was busy eating corn. Stump climbed over to where there was a square opening. He leaned over, and looked down inside.

It was very dark. He chattered, *"HELLOOO!"*

His voice came back, *"HELLOOO!"*

All of a sudden, as Stump stuck his head into the square
opening, he lost his balance, and fell into the darkness.

He didn't know he had fallen into a chimney. From his
wedged position, he looked up, and could see the sky

Stump's friend heard Stump chattering for help. He jumped on the roof, looked in the dark hole, and told Stump, "Use your claws, and push yourself to the top."

The man and the woman heard commotion inside the chimney. They went outside; and just as they looked up at the chimney, they saw a small head pop out. Stump was so happy to breathe the fresh air.

At first they were surprised,
but then the man and woman
laughed....

Later, down on the ground by their favorite tree, Stump's squirrel friend said, **"See what happens when you get too curious, and are not *careful?*"**

A week later, Stump and his squirrel friend had just finished eating breakfast. Stump was full of energy. He loved climbing trees. That day, he decided to climb a strange-looking tree that had *very thin branches.*

Stump climbed up onto a round metal object
on the strange-looking tree. He did not
realize that the object was an *electric
transformer,* and that the very thin branches
were *high-voltage electric wires.*

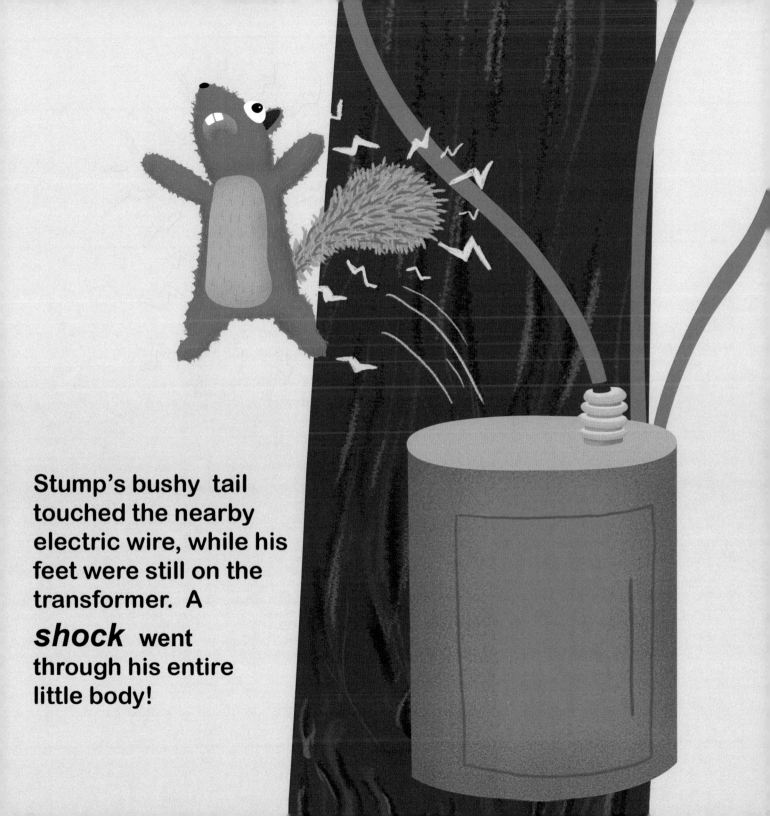

Stump's bushy tail touched the nearby electric wire, while his feet were still on the transformer. A **shock** went through his entire little body!

Stump fell to the ground.

Shadow, the donkey, saw what happened; and walked over to the fence. He looked down at Stump. "Are you alright, little buddy?"

Stump's squirrel friend also ran over, and looked at his friend, who sat dazed and confused.

When Stump finally got up, his friends looked
at him with wide eyes and their mouths open.
There, next to Stump,

was his *tail!*

Stump turned to see what his friends were looking at. He saw his very own tail lying on the ground.

Stump began to cry. He was always *so proud* of his beautiful tail. Stump's squirrel friend exclaimed,
"The electric wire must have burned it off!"

Stump's squirrel friend put his arm around Stump,
and he said in a gentle voice,
"Stump, next time,

look before you leap."

Many days went by before Stump could jump and climb. Finally, his little stump healed. Stump had learned his lesson:

Now, he *ALWAYS* waits for the birds to scatter the seeds before eating his meal. He is a lot more careful about looking into dark holes on the tops of houses. He is also very busy climbing trees; and he is *ALWAYS* careful of the branches he chooses to explore.

Now, Stump ALWAYS

LOOKS BEFORE HE LEAPS.

Author

Barbara Gensch, married to Author, Editor, and Mechanical Engineering Specialist, Larry D. Gensch, has ALWAYS loved children. She and Larry raised their three children, Tammy, Richard, and Daniel in the Midwest; and later moved to Texas. In Texas, Barbara, as a Preschool Teacher for seventeen years, read stories to all the children of her school. "I loved to animate the characters. When I walked in the door of a classroom, the children would run to me, yelling, 'Read stories! Read stories!' I eventually became known as 'The Book Lady.'"

Illustrator

Recently graduated from the University of Minnesota—Duluth, Rosie Lin is a digital designer, living and working in Plymouth, Minnesota. In her free time, she enjoys many hobbies, including snowboarding, polymer clay sculpting, photography, and of course, illustrating. Her favorite thing about illustrating is seeing a project evolve from thoughtful text, to scrappy sketches, to fully-formed compositions.

The End

Made in the USA
Columbia, SC
30 May 2021